Something Magic

Something Magic

❧ ❧

by Maggie S. Davis

illustrated by Mary O'Keefe Young

Simon & Schuster Books for Young Readers

Published by Simon & Schuster
New York · London · Toronto · Sydney · Tokyo · Singapore

SIMON & SCHUSTER BOOKS FOR YOUNG READERS
Simon & Schuster Building, Rockefeller Center, 1230 Avenue of the Americas,
New York, New York 10020
Text copyright © 1991 by Maggie S. Davis
Illustrations copyright © 1991 by Mary O'Keefe Young

SIMON & SCHUSTER BOOKS FOR YOUNG READERS is a trademark of Simon & Schuster.
Designed by Lucille Chomowicz
Manufactured in the United States of America   10   9   8   7   6   5   4   3   2   1

Library of Congress Cataloging-in-Publication Data. Davis, Maggie S., 1942-   Something
magic / by Maggie S. Davis ; illustrated by Mary O'Keefe Young.   p.   cm.   Summary: A
summer visit to Gammy's place in the country evokes the magic of blueberries and moonlight, a magic strong enough to overcome the sorrow of a lost kitten or the absence of
Grandpa.
[1. Grandmothers—Fiction.]   I. Young, Mary O'Keefe, ill.   II. Title.   PZ7.D2952So
1991   [E]—dc20   90-10062   ISBN 0-671-69627-0

loved my grandmother. "Gammy" I called her. Everyone said we looked just alike.

Summers, I stayed at Gammy's in a room on the top floor. The ceiling there was blue and slanted almost to my pillow.

There were chickens to feed at Gammy's, and a cow to milk, and blueberries to rake for pie and jam. I liked raking blueberries. Sometimes my friend Hannah helped me.

One Sunday, Gammy served me breakfast in bed on a tray. She sat beside me, and my kitten kept us company. I smelled the rose Gammy brought me and wondered just which part of her I looked like.

Not her eyes—they were wider set than mine. And her hair was white, as if snow had just fallen. Mine was brown, with gold running through on sunny days. Gammy called it my stardust hair. She said it glittered even in the moonlight.

After breakfast, we dug clams. The mist swirled around
us like steam rising from a cooling kettle.

"My legs don't move as fast as yours," Gammy teased me.
"Maybe they need some oil!"

We lifted our skirts to wade then. Blue lines ran down
Gammy's legs like tiny rivers. My legs were smooth
and tan.

"My grandmother canoed in this cove—Indians did, too,"
Gammy told me. "Your grandpa fished just beyond," she
said, "before the sea got him."

"Remember what Grandpa used to tell us?" I asked her.
"'If you wake up in the morning and nothing hurts, it's
going to be a good day.'"

Gammy threw her head back and laughed with me,
as loud as Grandpa would have laughed if he'd been
listening.

When lunch was over, I couldn't find my kitten. I ran and ran looking for him—around the cove, up through the woods beyond the blueberry fields, down the hill toward the sea.

"Zoot!" I shouted. "Where are you?"

I called him till my throat hurt. Then I cried myself to sleep behind the schoolhouse.

Gammy found me. The moon was up, and it lit our way home.

"Zoot!" we kept calling. "Zoot!" But Zoot never came.

The next summer, I asked Gammy if she
remembered him.

Gammy's face went soft. She dropped the
sheet she'd been hanging and looked at me.
"I remember how you missed him," she said.

"The way you missed Grandpa?" I asked her.
"The way I still do," she told me. "Some days,"
she said, "I look all around and feel him with me."
"So do I," I said. "And know what?"
"What?" Gammy whispered.
"I feel Zoot with me, too," I said.

Gammy tucked me close. She ruffled my hair. "Quick! Quick!" she whooped to cheer me up. "Get out the crayons before we lose the light!" I did, and met her by the willow.

"You use the red crayon first if you want to," Gammy told me. She smelled like the lemons she'd sliced for our tea.

While I was coloring shoes and Gammy was coloring socks, our knuckles bumped. Mine looked like dimples. Gammy's looked like small stones.

That night, before I went to sleep, Gammy wanted to see how much I'd grown. I tried to stretch taller than I really was, but I couldn't fool her. When I stretched, Gammy stretched, too.

"Good night," I told her when I'd climbed into bed. She was sitting in the wide, stuffed chair beside my window.

"Good night, yourself!" she said. Then she smiled at me, and something magic happened.

Light shone from inside her. It twinkled in her eyes and
made her face look rosy. It was brighter than the moon
and made me warm.

Maybe that's the part of Gammy that I look like.

Maybe that's the part of you that looks like me.